For Ella
– C.R.

For Apolline
– A.S.

First published 2021 by Nosy Crow Ltd
The Crow's Nest, 14 Baden Place, Crosby Row
London SE1 1YW

Nosy Crow Eireann Ltd
44 Orchard Grove, Kenmare, Co Kerry V93 FY22, Ireland

www.nosycrow.com

ISBN 978 1 83994 319 5 (HB)
ISBN 978 1 83994 500 7 (PB)

Nosy Crow and associated logos are trademarks and/or registered
trademarks of Nosy Crow Ltd

Text © Camilla Reid 2021
Illustrations © Axel Scheffler 2021

A CIP catalogue record for this book is available from the British Library.

Printed in China

5 7 9 8 6 4 (HB)
1 3 5 7 9 8 6 4 2 (PB)

Pip and Posy

www.pipandposybooks.com

Pip and Posy

The Birthday Party

Written by

Camilla Reid

Illustrated by

Axel Scheffler

nosy crow

It was Posy's birthday.
She was very excited.

Just then, the doorbell rang.

"Happy Birthday, Posy!" said Pip.

He had brought Posy
a lovely present.

"A bus!" said Posy.

"Thank you so much, Pip!"

The bus was lots of fun.

But soon it was time for the party games.

First, they played musical statues…

then keep-the-balloons-in-the-air…

hide-and-seek...

and, last of all,
pin-the-tail-on-the-dinosaur!

Then it was
teatime.

Soon, Pip had a very special
surprise for Posy.

It was a beautiful birthday cake!

But as Pip was walking to the table,
he stepped on the bus.

Pip flew into the air...

and so did
the cake!

Poor Pip.

Poor Posy.

Poor cake.

Oh dear, oh dear, oh DEAR!

"I'm sorry, Posy," said Pip.
"Your cake is ruined."

"But it wasn't your fault, Pip," sniffed Posy.
"It was an accident."

They decided to tidy up.

And soon everything looked much better.

Then Pip had a good idea.

"Let's make new cakes," he said.

And that's what they did.

They made new cakes for everybody.

And THREE for Posy!

Happy birthday, Posy!

Hooray!